Places in Our Community

Our Community Center

by Lisa J. Amstutz

PEBBLE
a capstone imprint

Pebble Plus is published by Pebble, an imprint of Capstone.
1710 Roe Crest Drive, North Mankato, Minnesota 56003
www.capstonepub.com

Library of Congress Cataloging-in-Publication data is available on the Library of Congress website.
ISBN 978-1-9771-1259-0 (library binding)
ISBN 978-1-9771-1265-1 (paperback)
ISBN 978-1-9771-1766-3 (eBook PDF)

Summary: The community center is an important part of our community. Lots of people work together to make our community center a great place to be. Readers will learn about who works at the community center, what the workers do, and what makes a community center special. Simple, at-level text and vibrant photos help readers learn all about community centers.

Editorial Credits
Editor: Mari Schuh; Designers: Kay Fraser and Ashlee Suker; Media Researcher: Eric Gohl;
Production Specialist: Katy LaVigne

Photo Credits
Alamy: Hero Images Inc., 5, TongRo Images, 7; iStockphoto: FatCamera, 13, 15, 19, 21, Wavebreakmedia, 1; Newscom: ZUMA Press/Michael A. Jones, 9; Shutterstock: 1989studio, 22, Alexxndr, 2 (notebooks), barrirret, 4, 6, 8, 10, 12, 14, 16, 18, 20, Betelgejze, 3, BRG.photography, cover, Happy Together, 24, Microgen, 17, Monkey Business Images, 11, Pumm Amornrat, back cover, 2 (tiles), 23

Note to Parents and Teachers

The Places in Our Community set supports national social studies standards related to people, places, and environments. This book describes and illustrates a community center and the people who work there. The images support early readers in understanding the text. The repetition of words and phrases helps early readers learn new words. This book also introduces early readers to subject-specific vocabulary words, which are defined in the Glossary section. Early readers may need assistance to read some words and to use the Table of Contents, Glossary, Read More, Internet Sites, Critical Thinking Questions, and Index sections of the book.

All internet sites appearing in back matter were available and accurate when this book was sent to press.

Printed and bound in China.
002493

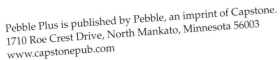

Table of Contents

Let's Visit a Community Center!

A community center is a place where people learn and play. They exercise too. Lots of people work at a community center. Let's meet some of them!

5

Who Works at a Community Center?

Hello! A receptionist

greets everyone. He signs up

people for activities and shows

them where to go. He answers

the phone and sends messages.

Who's in charge of the center?
The director! She hires workers
and plans new activities.
She answers questions
that workers have.

Good morning! A teacher greets her class. She helps people learn English at the center. Another class learns how to save money.

Tweet! Tweet! A coach blows his whistle. He teaches kids new skills. He helps players do their best. Go, team!

A fitness instructor leads
an exercise class.
The class works hard
and has fun. Exercise helps
people stay healthy.

Splash! This center has a pool. Swim teachers help kids learn to swim. Lifeguards make sure people are safe and follow the rules.

Time for camp!
Kids come to the center
each day. A camp counselor
leads hikes and other activities.
He plans art and science projects.

Healthy Communities

Community center workers have important jobs. They help people learn and grow. They help keep the community strong and healthy.

Glossary

exercise—a physical activity done to stay healthy and fit

fitness—a person's health and strength

lifeguard—a person trained to help swimmers

receptionist—someone whose job is to greet visitors and answer phone calls

rule—an instruction telling people what to do; rules help people learn, stay healthy, and stay safe.

whistle—an object that makes a high, loud sound

Read More

Emminizer, Theresa. *You're Part of a Neighborhood Community!* New York: Gareth Stevens, 2020.

Evans, Shira. *Helpers in Your Neighborhood.* Washington, D.C.: National Geographic Children's Books, 2018.

Nagle, Jeanne. *What is a Community?* New York: Britannica Educational Publishing, 2017.

Internet Sites

Fact Monster: Coach
https://www.factmonster.com/cool-stuff/jobs-involving-sports/coach

People, Occupations, Jobs, and Community from Enchanted Learning
https://www.enchantedlearning.com/themes/communityhelpers.shtml

Community Club from Scholastic
http://teacher.scholastic.com/commclub/

Critical Thinking Questions

1. Who greets people when they enter a community center?

2. Name two sports kids could play at a community center.

3. What kinds of classes might people take at a community center?

Index